This Little Hippo
book belongs to

Scholastic Children's Books,
Commonwealth House, 1-19 New Oxford Street,
London WC1A 1NU, UK
a division of Scholastic Ltd

London ~ New York ~ Toronto ~ Sydney ~ Auckland

First published by Scholastic Ltd, 1998

Developed from the original book The Night After Christmas,
by James Stevenson. The Forgotten Toys is an animated series produced
by Hibbert Ralph Entertainment for Link Entertainment,
scripted by Mark Holloway,
directed by Graham Ralph and produced by Karen Davidsen.
Executive producers David Hamilton and Claire Derry.
Script adaptation by Norman Redfern. Book illustrations by Les Gibbard.

2 4 6 8 10 9 7 5 3 1

ISBN 0 590 19976 5

Printed in Belgium by Proost

The Forgotten Toys

On the Road

Once upon a time, when they were far away from home, a little girl and her brother lost their favourite toys . . . and the toys didn't like being lost. Now Teddy, and Annie the ragdoll, were on their way home, but the journey back to their children was long and full of adventures.

Teddy and Annie were riding in the back of a lorry which was rattling down a bumpy road. They were a long way from home, and Teddy wasn't happy.

"Sprouts!" he complained. "You had to pick a sprout truck, didn't you?"

"It's going in the right direction," Annie pointed out.

"We'd be better off walking," moaned Teddy.

"That's not what you said when we were walking," Annie reminded him.

The lorry was stopping.

"I'm off!" announced Teddy.

He scrambled over the mound of sprouts and found the lever which opened the back of the lorry.

"Teddy, don't . . ." said Annie.

But Teddy did. The door fell open, and the mountain of sprouts tumbled out, taking Annie and Teddy with it. Spud, a fierce bull terrier, watched the sprouts rolling towards him across the car-park. He growled, but the sprouts kept coming. So did Teddy. The tide of sprouts carried him smack into Spud's face.

"Sorry," muttered Teddy.

"You will be," replied Spud.

Teddy tried to run away, and Spud tried to chase him, but there were sprouts everywhere. They lost their footing and skidded to a halt at the feet of a very large truck driver, who looked even fiercer than Spud. The driver reached down, picked up Spud with one hand, and Teddy with the other, and stomped back to his dumper truck.

"Oh, no!" sighed Annie, from under a pile of sprouts.

"Spud hates toys," growled the dog.

The driver put Spud on the passenger seat and slammed the door.

"You don't scare me!" jeered Teddy through the window.

As he passed the front of his truck, the driver stopped, and tied Teddy to the bars in front of the engine.

"He'll make a nice mascot," grinned the driver.

He climbed into his cab, turned the key, and the engine started throbbing behind Teddy.

"H - e - l - l - l - pp!" he stammered.

Annie scrambled off the sprout heap and ran across the car park. She tried to grab Teddy, but she couldn't reach him. The dumper truck started to move. There was a chain dangling from the back of the lorry. Annie caught hold of it and hauled herself aboard. She landed, exhausted, in a pile of sand.

Teddy held his paws in front of his eyes as the truck thundered down the road. The journey seemed to take forever, but at last they stopped.

"Get me down!" yelled Teddy. Spud jumped out of the cab and tried to snap at him, but Teddy was just out of reach.

"On second thoughts," Teddy decided, "I'll stay here!"

They were in a building site. The driver pulled a lever in his cab, and the rear part of the truck tilted upwards and backwards. The sand flowed out, taking Annie with it. The driver climbed down and began shovelling the sand. What was that on his spade? "Great! Another mascot for my truck," he said, pushing Annie into the gap next to Teddy.

"Where have you been?" Teddy asked her.

"Trying to help you," replied Annie.

"Help me?" Teddy repeated. "After all that's happened to me? Now you're stuck too."

"No, I'm not," said Annie, sliding out again. "By the way, what's that smell?"

Teddy sniffed. Something behind him was burning . . . his behind was burning!

"Help!" he cried. "I'm on fire!"

Annie pulled Teddy with all her might. He popped out and rushed away to cool off in the nearest puddle.

"You can't sit there, Teddy," said Annie. "Look!"
Teddy turned round. Spud was on his way!
"Run!" shouted Teddy.
Annie and Teddy raced across the building site. Spud was close behind them. With a ferocious growl, he leapt through the air. Teddy and Annie dived to the ground, and Spud flew over their heads. In front of him, the lorry driver had just finished laying a new concrete path. Splat! Spud landed smack in the middle of the path. The driver was furious!

Teddy and Annie turned and ran, but Spud was too quick for them. They were cornered, in a dead-end, and there was only one way out.

"The ladder!" cried Teddy. "He can't follow us up there!" Teddy started to climb up the ladder. Annie followed, but Spud was already snapping at her feet. In a panic, she grabbed the end of a rope, that was hanging nearby. She swung out of reach just in time.

"Spud hates toys," growled the dog.

"Why?" asked Annie.

"Because toys don't get sent out to work," said Spud, angrily. "Toys don't get hit with sticks. Toys don't get chained up and left out all night in the rain."

"Is that what your owner does to you?" asked Annie.

"Of course it is," said Spud, "and Spud don't like it."

Spud's owner, the truck driver, had a nasty temper. All that growling and snarling was getting on his nerves.

"Oi!" he shouted. "Come here!"

Spud slunk back to his owner.

"Don't hit Spud," pleaded the dog.

"Let's clear off, Pigtails," said Teddy.

"We can't leave him," said Annie. "He needs our help."

"Why should we help him?" asked Teddy.

The driver chained Spud to his truck. He was going to teach that dog a lesson.

"That's why," explained Annie pointing to Spud.

"What am I supposed to do?" asked Teddy.

"You distract the man," said Annie. "I'll rescue Spud."

She set off towards the terrified dog. Teddy looked around the building site. There must be something he could use . . .

"The bulldozer!" cried Teddy and ran towards it.

Annie crawled towards Spud.

"Spud, we'll save you," she whispered. "I'll untie you when he's not looking."

The driver was on his way. He was carrying a big stick.

"Hurry up, Teddy!" called Annie.

The lorry driver stood over Spud and raised the stick. Then he stopped and looked around. A bulldozer was rumbling over the building site, and it was coming towards him – fast! He dropped the stick and started running. Quickly, Annie unfastened Spud's chain.

"Come with us," she said. "We'll help you."

Spud's owner ran away across the site, and the bulldozer trundled after him. Teddy was at the controls, but he wasn't in control. He tried to stop, he tried to turn, he tried to slow down, but the bulldozer just went faster and faster.

"Help!" he shouted. "Pigtails!"

Annie and Spud watched Teddy thunder past.

"Will you help me, now?" asked Annie.

"Yes" said Spud. "Jump on!"

Annie climbed on to Spud's back.

"Follow that bulldozer!" she cried.

The bulldozer was heading towards a parked concrete mixer lorry. Spud raced after it, and ran alongside while Annie reached across to Teddy.

"Give me your paw," she shouted.

Teddy leapt from the speeding bulldozer just in time. It smashed into the back of the mixer truck.

Spud's owner stopped running and breathed a sigh of relief. He was safe at last. Suddenly, the mixer tipped over and poured concrete all over him. He stood there for a moment, covered from head to toe, and then he burst into tears.

Spud smiled.
"Spud don't hate toys no more," he said. "Toys are Spud's friends."
He licked Teddy's face.
"Get off!" spluttered Teddy.
"Come with us," said Annie. "We'll find you somewhere new to live."

The old farm truck rattled down a country lane. In the back, Teddy was complaining again.

"Why does every truck we get a lift in have to be full of sprouts?" he moaned.

"You mean you don't like sprouts?" Annie teased. "You never mentioned it before."

The farmer reached across to the passenger seat and patted his new friend. Spud wagged his tail happily. He had found his new home.